KIDS CAN'T STOP READING
THE CHOOSE YOUR
OWN ADVENTURE® STORIES!

"Choose Your Own Adventure is the best thing that has come along since books themselves."

—Alysha Beyer, age 11

"I didn't read much before, but now I read my Choose Your Own Adventure books almost every night."

—Chris Brogan, age 13

"I love the control I have over what happens next."

—Kosta Efstathiou, age 17

"Choose Your Own Adventure books are so much fun to read and collect—I want them all!"

—Brendan Davin, age 11

And teachers like this series, too:

"We have read and reread, worn thin, loved, loaned, bought for others, and donated to school libraries our Choose Your Own Adventure books."

CHOOSE YOUR OWN ADVENTURE®—
AND MAKE READING MORE FUN!

D0802034

Bantam Books in the Choose Your Own Adventure® series
Ask your bookseller for the books you have missed

THE SECRET OF MYSTERY HILL

BY DOUG WILHELM

ILLUSTRATED BY TOM LA PADULA

An R.A. Montgomery Book

BANTAM BOOKS
NEW YORK · TORONTO · LONDON · SYDNEY · AUCKLAND

RL4, age 10 and up

THE SECRET OF MYSTERY HILL

A Bantam Book/November 1993

*CHOOSE YOUR OWN ADVENTURE® is a registered
trademark of Bantam Books,
a division of Bantam Doubleday Dell Publishing Group, Inc.
Registered in U.S. Patent and Trademark Office and elsewhere.*

Original conception of Edward Packard

*Cover art by Bill Schmidt
Interior illustrations by Tom La Padula*

ISBN 0-553-56001-8

Published simultaneously in the United States and Canada

Bantam Books are published by Bantam Books, a division of
Bantam Doubleday Dell Publishing Group, Inc. Its trademark,
consisting of the words "Bantam Books" and the portrayal of a
rooster, is Registered in U.S. Patent and Trademark Office and
in other countries. Marca Registrada. Bantam Books, 1540
Broadway, New York, New York 10036.

PRINTED IN THE UNITED STATES OF AMERICA

OPM   0 9 8 7 6 5 4 3 2 1

AUTHOR'S NOTE

The Secret of Mystery Hill is a work of fiction, but Mystery Hill itself is based on a very real place. Located in North Salem, New Hampshire, the strange stone complex known as America's Stonehenge is steeped in history, legend—and possibility. Was it really built by British colonists centuries before Columbus came to the New World? How? Why? We may never know for sure, but hundreds of curious people come each year to explore this fascinating place, taking great care not to disturb the fragile ruins. Perhaps after reading this book you'll visit, too.

For Corey D. Wilhelm

WARNING!!!

Do not read this book straight through from beginning to end. These pages contain many different adventures that you may have when you encounter the strange powers of Mystery Hill. From time to time as you read along, you will be asked to make a choice. Your choice may lead to success or disaster!

The adventures you have are the results of your choices. You are responsible because you choose. After you make a decision, follow the instructions to find out what happens to you next.

Think carefully before you act. Mystery Hill is no ordinary pile of rocks, and the people and places you find may not be as they seem. Many lives—including your own—may depend on your quick thinking and good judgment.

Good luck!

Last fall you moved with your family to North Salem, a small town in the wooded hills of southern New Hampshire. Now and then during the school year you've heard people mention a place called Mystery Hill.

It's a small hill in the woods, covered with tunnels and chambers and walls of rock. Some people say it's been there since before Columbus. You definitely don't believe that. You don't even bother to look for Mystery Hill until one day, the last day in April, your class goes there on a field trip.

The place is now a small tourist attraction, with a parking lot and a little building with a snack bar. You're looking forward to getting back to that snack bar. You and your classmates walk around to the back of the building, where a path leads into the woods. An old man wearing a plaid flannel shirt and sporting a white beard meets your group.

"My name is Merrill," the old man says. "I'll be your guide to Mystery Hill. I think you'll find it a very special place."

He says that to everyone in the group—but then he turns and looks right at *you*. His eyes are blue. He smiles.

You smile back, but you shudder. Why has he singled you out?

Merrill starts up the path. "Let's get started."

Turn to page 2.

The path is a little muddy, but it's not a long walk. Laughing and fooling around, your group tromps up a gentle slope among the just-budding trees. The old guide pays no attention to your antics—he just walks ahead.

Suddenly you see a strange jumble of shapes on a low, open hill up ahead. At first they look like a random bunch of big rocks. But then you see walls and round shapes and dark openings like small doorways. Everything is built of old, mottled gray stones.

Forgetting the others, even old Merrill, you stride ahead, mesmerized. This is unlike any other place you've ever seen.

Go on to the next page.

Merrill shows your group around. Mystery Hill is actually a complex of ancient stone structures. The low doorways lead into rectangular chambers where the ceilings are made of awesomely large stones, precisely fitted together. You peer into a deep, stone-lined shaft.

"That's the Well of the Crystals," Merrill says. "It is believed that crystals were sources of great power to these people."

In the center of the complex is a broad, flat rock set up on smaller rocks like a table. A shallow groove is cut around its sides, close to the rim, as if to drain away liquid.

You shudder again, wondering what the rock was for.

Most of your classmates are still fooling around. But your curiosity mounts. You have a strange, important feeling about this place—as if you were meant to come here.

Turn to page 48.

You start to wave your arms in protest, but it's no use. You run, but the horses come pounding up behind. Stumbling, you turn in terror.

The Briton's face contorts in fury as he lifts his sword to strike. You raise your bare arms, pedaling backward. Then your foot touches air, and you're falling.

The Britons peer over the edge, and they grow smaller as the air rushes by. You're falling —you stepped off the path . . .

Your body bounces off a rock outcrop, and you lose consciousness. You don't know it or feel it as you tumble a thousand feet to your final resting place, among the old mountains in the country of Cymru, now known as Wales.

The End

You'd love a chance to serve Arthur personally, but you know he would appreciate your willingness to serve in battle.

"I'll carry that flag," you say.

"Come quickly, then," says Merrill. He dismounts and leads you to a dark-haired man who sits on a horse nearby. The man's breastplate and his horse's saddle blanket are decorated with a gold rooster on a crimson background.

"Nyall," says Merrill, "here is your standard-bearer."

The dark-haired man turns and looks you over. He has brightly dancing eyes. He grins.

"You'll have a chance to prove yourself this morning," he says to you, as if he knows that's your task. "But I'll have no wild antics from you. Take this standard." He reaches for the pole, stuck in the ground, and hands it to you. "Carry this by my side—always by my side. If I charge ahead, you come quickly behind, holding the standard high. In the midst of battle my fighters must always know where I am. Understand?"

You nod. Nyall turns from you and peers through the trees. Down below, the path is full of Saxons. You take your place at Nyall's side.

Go on to the next page.

Now a trumpet's sound pierces the forest. With one great yell, the Britons charge from the trees down at the startled Saxons.

"Warriors of Avalon," shouts Nyall as the wave breaks downward. "Stay with me!"

Holding the gold rooster high, you sprint after Nyall's gray horse. You're going into battle—in the name of Arthur.

Turn to page 46.

8

Late that night you sneak out of your house and ride your bike to Mystery Hill. The moon is out, and you find your way easily along the path through the woods.

A tall green wire fence surrounds the complex. The gate is locked, but you scale the fence easily. Not really knowing why you're here, you lie down on the platform, gazing up at the stars, waiting.

A few hours later, you wake up. It's still dark, but early dawn glows over the distant horizon. You blink and realize Merrill is standing over you. He is wearing a dark, rough robe. He holds a small chunk of crystal.

"Once in a great while," he tells you, "this place chooses a voyager."

You nod.

Merrill continues. "At sunrise you will begin your journey. This crystal will take you." He presses the rough stone into your hand. It is colorless in the gray of the coming dawn.

"Where am I going?" you ask.

Merrill looks into your eyes again. "Only you can make that choice," he tells you. "You can join the May Day ritual at the Dawn of Mystery Hill. Or you may venture to the time of the Great Heroes, where kings and brave warriors fight side by side."

Go on to the next page.

If you go to the Dawn of Mystery Hill, you think, you could unlock the secrets of this four-thousand-year-old puzzle. But what if strangers are not welcome at such a sacred ritual? Or, if you choose otherwise, are you worthy to become one of the Great Heroes?

The sky is getting lighter. "Hurry!" urges Merrill. "You must choose!"

If you join the May Day ritual at Mystery Hill, turn to page 71.

If you choose the time of the Great Heroes, turn to page 58.

When you wake up, all you know is how much your head hurts. You'd kill for a couple of aspirin.

Then you open your eyes.

It is totally silent here. You look around, stunned, at the scene in the cleft between the mountains. Countless dead and dying men lie heaped and tangled up with each other. They are Britons and Saxons both; some have died in pairs, gripping each other, swords and battle-axes plunged deeply into each other's lifeless bodies.

Not a soul is moving. You turn and see with horror the form of Nyall, still pinned beneath his horse. The chieftain's face is gray. His eyes are lifeless. You turn away. Your mouth is dry.

Is this real? Why is everything so still, so silent? You cannot hear a groan or even a crow's call. Where are the birds, the crows, and vultures to pick over the dead? Where did the armies go?

Where is Merrill?

You sit up straight. You look up the steep hill —but you see only forest. *Where did he go?* How can you get back home without him?

Then you hear his voice. "Meet me on the Island of the Heroes."

The *what*?

You look back up the hill, in the direction of the voice. But you see nothing.

Turn to page 106.

12

Dawn is about to break in the east. As you watch, the Saxons march into view below.

They are big, rough-clad men. They wear leather tunics and carry fat swords and round shields made of metal-studded wood. Rhythmically they pound on the shields with the heels of their swords.

The Britons around you stand tense and rigid. Hidden among these trees, they wait while the whole Saxon force—spread out thinly along the mountain trail—ribbons into view at your feet.

Merrill draws you back. "This is the last great battle that Arthur's forces will wage on the Saxons," he whispers. "You may play a part at this moment in history, but you must choose which part. The fighters closest to us need a standard-bearer to carry their pennant into the battle." He points to a red flag nearby with the gold figure of a crowing rooster.

"This is a dangerous, important task. You must stay with this group's battle chief and carry the flag where he orders in the fight. Or else you can hurry to the command post. Arthur needs a dependable messenger."

Dawn is breaking over the Scottish hills. The warriors of Britain are ready to attack.

But before you make your choice, there's something you must ask this mysterious old man.

Turn to page 54.

You realize the other warriors would never hear your call over the deafening battle. You run the few yards to Nyall. You hop over dying Britons and Saxons, dodging the deadly sweep of swords and the tumbling struggles of men who hammer and stab at each other.

As you reach Nyall you realize you've got another awful choice. You want to reach down and try to help the chieftain free himself from the dying, thrashing horse. But your orders are to hold the standard high. Should you follow them and just stand there? Or should you stoop down and try to help?

If you follow orders and hold the standard high, turn to page 67.

If you try to help Nyall get free, turn to page 53.

But the axe is heavy, and his swing is slow. You duck, he misses, and you dart to the stone platform with the man close behind. You raise your crystal to the sun. The sun's top half, glowing red, has risen above the distant hill.

Is it too late? Will the crystal work?

You hear the man struggling behind you to climb onto the platform. You bend down and grab the axe, wrenching it free. You raise it. The robed man cringes. He falls to the ground beneath the platform, cowering there.

"You murderous coward," you say.

With your free hand, you raise the crystal to the sun. It glows orange, then fiery red. Warmth travels down your arm and erupts inside you.

The power this time is tremendous, and you're shaking as if you'll come apart. Everything explodes in brilliant light. You fall to the floor, the crystal tumbling away.

Turn to page 23.

16

You can't pass up the chance to meet Arthur face-to-face.

"I'll serve Arthur," you say.

"Fine," says Merrill. "Now we take leave of these men."

The horse heads off among the old trees, leaving behind the colorful line of British warriors. As if it knows where to go, the animal makes its way well into the forest, deep among the shadows.

You enter a clearing. The early-morning light falls on multicolored tents. Your horse steps up to the largest tent, one with broad stripes of green and gold. You and Merrill dismount and step in.

Inside is a broad-shouldered, handsome man with reddish-brown hair and beard. He wears a fine tunic of green, threaded with gold. This is the great Arthur.

The Britons' chief nods to Merrill. Arthur's unsmiling face seems deeply troubled.

"The message has come," he tells Merrill. "It is as you foretold."

You look at Merrill. *What* did he foretell?

Go on to the next page.

Gravely Merrill nods. "Here is your messenger," he tells Arthur.

"You must accompany him," Arthur says. "Mordred—that slime-bellied reptile—still respects and fears you."

Merrill nods. "I will go."

You look from Arthur to Merrill, but neither gives you any clue. Go where? And who is Mordred?

Turn to page 68.

You will tell the ferryman you wish to travel by water.

Your path comes to a rough wooden pier beside the great bay. Nearby is a building made of timbers. A light burns inside. Out here it is chilly, and the gray waters of the bay scare you a little, lapping with the early-spring wind.

You dismount Mystery and walk out onto the pier. There's no ship here—only a small sailboat, bobbing on the water below these wood planks. The boat is built of rough planks that come to a point at either end. There's a single mast and a crumpled pile of cloth in the boat.

You hear a commotion behind you. You look up to see a thin, dark-haired man burst from the door of the building nearby. He is running this way, carrying a lumpy bag.

Now a stout man charges out of the building. He's chasing the thin man, shouting something. You stand there watching as the skinny man scampers onto the pier and runs right at you.

"Get in," he says, hopping into the boat.

"Are you the fer—"

"Get *in*," he hisses. He yanks a loop of rope from a post. The boat is free.

"But," you say, "I'm not . . ."

"A thief? Like me? Explain that to *him*."

You look back: The heavyset man is charging onto the pier. Behind a sandy beard, his face is fiery with anger. The only escape is by boat.

You jump in.

Turn to page 116.

Speedily and surely, Mystery glides through the forest and out across the British countryside. You wonder how the horse can seem to know just where it's going. It gallops along a road that's been carefully paved with rectangular stones. Weeds and tall grass grow between the stones. These must be Roman roads, you realize, untended since the fall of the empire.

You ride past farm carts loaded with planting tools. It's spring, and the fields are muddy. Here and there you pass castles—not the towered castles of storybooks but great rings of piled-up earth, fortified with big timbers. Some of these command the tops of hills.

One of those hill forts reveals to you the next sign of the Saxon invaders. You pass a bald hill from which black smoke pours. At its base a simple farm village has been burned. Its huts are charred ruins, its muddy lanes a mess of turned-over carts and slaughtered animals.

You see three blond men in rough clothes and high leather boots carrying round wooden shields. They're laughing and tromping around the village, dragging a dead pig. When they see you, they stop laughing, drop the pig, and charge toward the road.

Turn to page 100.

Some hours later you are walking, already leg-weary, along a narrow, rocky path high up in the mountains. You hear horses clopping behind you. You stop and wait for these people to approach.

From around a bend comes a small party of British warriors. You recognize their long shields, Roman-style breastplates, and slender swords. Maybe they're returning from the battle in Scotland.

You start to speak. But the lead Briton spots your round shield and stubby sword, and his face reddens with anger. He spurs his horse to charge at you.

He thinks you're a Saxon!

Turn to page 4.

22

You grab the sides of the table and push off. Your sneakers dig in, and you're sprinting through the stone maze. Two of the robed men try to grab you—but you fake and dodge the first with a football move, then crash through the second, sending him sprawling as you race for the trees. The deerskin-clad people stand watching at the edge of the woods.

Will they try to stop you? They could do that easily—they know these woods, and you don't.

You run for the trees, just a few yards away from the deerskin people. If they're going to chase you, they'll do it now.

Turn to page 104.

The floor is dark. It's made of wood.

You see a pair of leather boots and faded jeans. You look up. Merrill is bending over you.

"Didn't expect to see you back so soon," he says. "In fact, I didn't expect to see you back at all."

Anger surges inside you. "All they wanted was a victim—a human sacrifice," you say. "How could you let me go?"

Merrill shakes his head. "This place has much more power than any old man," he says. "I am simply an agent of that power. Mystery Hill itself chose you for this journey, and you alone chose where to go. I could not affect either one."

Your anger subsides, but you're still curious about one thing. "You said before that the Dawn of Mystery Hill was 'not your time.' What is your time?"

"A long, long time ago," Merrill answers.

"You're a lot older than you look, aren't you?"

Merrill smiles. "Yes, I am."

Something tells you that's all the information you're going to get from him. You guess you'll have to look up a few things at the library, but you know that no book can possibly tell the secret of Mystery Hill.

You stand up and dust yourself off. You can't help but smile as you wonder: Is that dust from today—or from the Bronze Age, some four thousand years ago?

The End

There's no heat—the coals of the great fire are already cool. At the head of the spread of black embers, you see something different. Dismounting, you walk right into the ashes to look.

Lying untouched, unburned and unblackened amid the charred bits, is the crystal. You pick it up and put it in your pocket.

"Trust the mystery." The voice is the red-haired woman's. You look up just in time to see her disappear, smiling, into the mist.

Trust the mystery. The Green Man said it, too.

As you walk out of the ruin, the land all around you is green. Grass has come up. Spring blossoms are everywhere.

Coming to the river again, you find a path alongside it this time. Rivers always run to the sea, don't they? You decide to follow this one there.

Turn to page 94.

Is it real? You rush to the horse, which shakes its head as if to greet you.

You pat its sides. It feels real enough. In the saddlebags are some bread, a blanket, and some unfamiliar coins. Your fingers search your jeans pocket for the crystal. It's still there.

The Island of the Heroes. You have to find it.

You mount the horse and pat its neck. "I'll call you Mystery," you whisper.

The horse carries you forward, through the Caledonia Woods.

Turn to page 20.

Eight days later you stand on the misty beach in Cornwall, the southwestern tip of Britain.

By the water, the broad spread of sand is lined with all the warriors of Britain. They now stand in two armies, facing each other. There are shields and breastplates and pennants and flags of every color. Horses stand proudly while swords, battle-axes, spears, and wood staffs are held ready.

You stand with Arthur's force. At your belt hangs a short, broad sword that Merrill gave you in Avalon.

But Arthur's and Mordred's men must not fight. If Briton clashes with Briton, here at the far edge of the island, Arthur's brave campaign against the Saxons will surely end in a bloody and pointless clash. It must not happen.

Turn to page 28.

"I will meet Mordred on the ground between our ranks and his," Arthur announces. "There must be no movement among the fighters—none. If even one raises a weapon, we may be powerless to avert a terrible clash."

You watch as Arthur rides forth, clad in his gold-threaded green, to meet the treacherous chieftain who has occupied his home. Still mounted, the two men confer.

You glance downward and see a snake. It has crawled from some dune grass behind you. You recognize it as an adder—extremely poisonous.

The snake is poised, its head quivering, a few inches from your foot, about to strike.

Should you draw your sword to kill the snake and save your own life? Or should you remain still, as Arthur ordered?

If you remain motionless, turn to page 103.

If you draw your sword, turn to page 38.

Your horse bursts from the Forest of Scotland and glides with magical speed across open farmland dotted with tiny, simple villages. Here and there smoke spirals up from villages that seem to be on fire.

"The work of Saxons," Merrill mutters, nodding toward a rising smudge of dark smoke. "They are the invaders, the new rulers of this land."

"But what about Arthur? Doesn't he fight the Saxons? Isn't he a great hero?"

"Yes and yes." Merrill nods. "But now he has his hands full with Mordred."

The ancient farm country rushes by. "Who is Mordred?" you ask, the air whistling in your ears.

"He was among the British chieftains whom Arthur thought loyal," Merrill says. "But when the Britons rode off on the campaign to Scotland, Mordred stayed behind. Arthur has received word that in his absence, Mordred has marched into Cammlatt, Arthur's own hilltop fortress. Now Arthur must turn his forces from the Saxons to respond."

"You mean the British might battle . . . themselves?"

Go on to the next page.

Merrill sighs. "We shall see," he says.

"Arthur said you foretold this," you say. "How did you know what would happen? Who are you, really?"

Merrill's eyes sparkle, but he does not answer your question. "Do you see those hills ahead?" he asks instead. "On the other side is the Vale of Avalon, home of Arthur's Cammlatt."

Turn to page 110.

You and Merrill are walking in a forest—but it's definitely not one in New Hampshire. These trees are very old, with massive trunks and spreading limbs. It's just before dawn once again —you can see the dim glow up ahead. You hear heavy steps beside Merrill. You look up to see that he's leading a horse.

The horse is tall and pale gray, with a polished leather saddle and saddlebags. Merrill is still wearing his long cloak—you can see it's a deep, dark blue. He reaches into the saddlebag and pulls out a simple, sleeveless tunic of stout cloth in long stripes of orange and red—the colors of sunrise.

"Wear this," the old man says. You pull the tunic over your sweatshirt. Merrill hands you a heavy belt of braided blue cloth with threads of gold. You tie it around your waist.

"Where are we?" you ask, mesmerized by the grandeur of the forest.

"In the Forest of Caledonia—southern Scotland," Merrill answers.

"When?"

"By your reckoning, the year is A.D. 460."

You whistle. "Cool," you say, grinning. "So what are we doing here?"

Turn to page 113.

34

Beside the dark-stained table is the low, outer wall of a stone chamber.

Now a voice begins to speak. A man's low, commanding tones come from beneath the table itself.

You don't understand the words, nor how the stone table can be talking. All around you the deerskin-clad people point and murmur. They are awestruck—and deeply frightened.

They must think it's magic, but you're sure it's trickery. You suspect someone is hiding behind that stone wall, inside that chamber.

The voice is chanting, louder and louder. It shouts some sort of command. The crowd catches its breath.

The men in ivory robes push you toward the stone slab. One of them reaches down and picks up an axe of hammered bronze.

Suddenly you understand. At the dawn of May Day, the voice from the table is demanding a sacrifice. The ridges in the table are cut to catch the victim's blood. The stone is stained by the blood of countless ritual murders.

And today's victim is you.

Turn to page 59.

The sail catches the wind and the little boat surges out into the bay. Suddenly you remember Mystery.

You look to shore; the horse is calmly trotting back toward Avalon. You pat your pocket. The crystal is there.

The man turns to you. "You won't need a horse where we're going," he says.

"Where *are* we going?"

His sharp eyes flicker. "Off around those mountains there's an island," he confides. "It's got a secret hiding place. People say it holds the treasures of heroes."

Your breath catches. You're going to the island.

But isn't this man a thief?

You can't let him go to the Island of the Heroes and plunder it!

Maybe your test is to fight this man. You consider drawing your sword.

But should you? How do you really know what his intentions are? Maybe you should just go along for now and see.

If you draw your sword,
turn to page 79.

If you go along with the sailor,
turn to page 118.

You figure you're more likely to be able to out-run the robed men than to convince the natives of the voice trick. You decide to bolt for the woods.

The man guides you to your knees beside the table. Slowly but firmly he pushes your head down until the side of your face presses against the cold stone. He leaves your hands and feet free.

Everyone else is just watching, as if they all expect you to submit. How do the white-robed men get this power? Whom do they sacrifice when they haven't got you?

The eerie voice from the table chants louder and louder. Now that you're close to it, you're sure it's really coming from inside the stone chamber beside you. The robed men have all turned toward the dawn, chanting along with the hidden voice.

The man beside you raises the bronze axe, letting go of your head to lift the heavy weapon.

Now!

Turn to page 22.

The snake does not seem ready to leave, so you draw your sword and slice off its head. Then you hear a shout.

One of Mordred's men has spotted your sword—and you look up to see his whole force charge. Arthur's men spur their horses and pound onto the sand. Caught in the middle, Arthur and Mordred draw their swords as the armies smash headlong into each other.

You watch, horrified, as men club, axe, and slice at each other. Helmets fly off. The air is shredded with the sickening sounds of horses screaming and men taking terrible wounds. A thick bank of mist rolls in from the sea, covering the bloody scene. Now you can see nothing—you only hear the terrible smashing, groaning, cursing, and gasping of dying men. In that fog, no one can know who is enemy and who is friend. Arthur's glory day is ending in a disaster even more hopeless than you'd feared.

Should you plunge into the fight? You stare, uncertain, at your sword.

"Don't."

The voice is Merrill's. You see the old man's shape, standing on a sand dune.

"Is it my fault?" you ask.

"No," says Merrill. "There was no changing this fate."

You stand in the mist until the terrible sounds of battle finally subside. The fog lifts—and what you see is the most awful thing of all.

Turn to page 112.

You raise the pole with its red pennant and gold rooster as high as you can. You wave it and shout:

"Warriors of Avalon!"

You look around, but the tangled combat writhes and stabs just the same. No one turns to look. You shout again, but your voice is lost in the shouting and screaming and pounding and crashing all around.

You look toward Nyall just as a Saxon rears his battle-axe above the chieftain's pinned body and brings it down. You turn away and walk, wobbly kneed, up the hill. Above you, you see Merrill turn his horse into the woods.

You run up the hill. You've got to catch up with Merrill. Only he knows how you can get back home! That is, if you *can* get back home at all.

The old man sits on the gray horse just inside the edge of the woods. He holds up his hand and, somehow, you cannot move.

"Now you must earn your choices," he says. "Find me on the Island of the Heroes."

With that he turns and disappears into the woods.

You rush after him, stumbling among the roots of the great old trees.

Then you stop. There before you, chewing some grass, stands the horse. Merrill is gone.

Turn to page 26.

40

You pound down the hall just ahead of the racing, exploding flames. You burst through the opening, and there's Mystery. You leap on the horse and shout, "Go, Mystery—fast!"

Mystery gallops away from the hall, then stops and turns around.

Flaming timbers fall away from the massive building as the roof collapses. It's a blazing inferno. In minutes, it's over. The great hall is nothing but a spread of charred black wood on the ground.

Mystery walks toward the ruins. You pull hard on the reins, trying to turn away, but the horse walks right up to the blackness.

Turn to page 25.

Tomah steps silently in his moccasins. You're almost as quiet in your sneakers. The two of you make your way through the woods until you see an opening and hear voices.

At the edge, Tomah motions for you to look. What you see makes you gasp.

You've studied the Native American people of New England—the Abenaki—in school. This is one of their villages.

Cooking fires burn outside two conical buildings covered with birchbark. Those are wigwams.

"Abenaki?" you ask.

Tomah's face widens in pleasure. "Abenaki!"

The name, you know, means "People of the Dawn Land."

In this village, women work around the fires while children cavort and play. But there are no men; they are all back at Mystery Hill.

Tomah motions for you to follow again. This time you're moving back toward the complex. Fear chills you, but you follow.

Tomah hides behind a rock. You look over it.

The stone complex is alive with work—and the workers are men clad in yellow deerskin.

They haul stones by hand and push big rocks on rollers made from the trunks of young trees. Watching over the workers, stern and commanding, are the white-robed men.

Turn to page 90.

Could the crystal you're carrying be the stone that the necklace is missing? Could the empty pendant have something to do with the barrenness all around—and with this woman's sickness?

Perhaps you should give them the crystal.

Give it to them? You need that crystal to get home. You can't give it away!

And if it belongs on this woman's neck, why do you have it in the first place? How did it get to Mystery Hill? And how come you never understand anything that's going on around here?

But maybe that's why you're here—to bring back the crystal.

Everyone is staring at you. They're waiting for something.

*If you don't mention the crystal,
turn to page 101.*

*If you offer it,
turn to page 82.*

Deep in the night, you and Tomah creep silently through the woods toward the stone complex that centuries in the future will be called Mystery Hill.

Through signs, Tomah has told you there will be another ceremony—another sacrifice—this dawn.

You're going to make that impossible, if you can.

During the day, you spied the bronze axe leaning against the sacrificial rock. You're hoping it's still there.

The moon is full. In its pale light the strange stone shapes around you are ghostly and unsettling. You and Tomah slip from the trees to the first stone wall. Then silently, slowly, moving in a crouch, you enter the complex.

There seem to be no guards. You move inward, all your senses alert for danger. You creep up to the awful guttered table.

The axe is not there.

You look at Tomah and shrug. He motions toward the door of the stone chamber—the one from which someone, you're sure, made the table "talk."

You point in there, chop, and shrug. *Is the axe in that chamber?*

Tomah nods.

You two crawl inside.

Go on to the next page.

It's pitch-black in here—you can see only the moonlit opening behind you. You crawl along the walls, hoping somehow to find the axe. You wonder if this is hopeless.

You hear a scrape. You turn to see the moonlit opening go dark.

In blackness you crawl to it. Someone has blocked the opening with a stone. It won't move.

You're trapped.

Turn to page 52.

46

As the Britons sweep down the hill in a wide rush of color, the sun breaks east of the Scottish mountains, suddenly glinting and shining off the warriors' armor and swords. You see Saxons shield their eyes, and you understand why the brilliant Arthur attacked at dawn. Then the wave of Arthur's fighters crashes into the Saxons.

You see Nyall ahead as he plunges into the attack. You sprint to catch up. As you rush down the slope, the scene in front of you turns crazy.

Turn to page 108.

"Who *were* these people?" you ask Merrill.

"Scientific carbon dating tests have proved that Mystery Hill is about four thousand years old," Merrill tells your class. "That's more than three thousand years before Columbus 'discovered' America. It's believed that the complex was built by people from ancient Britain. There are chambers like this in that country, too—and calendar stones."

"Calendar stones?" you echo.

The old man leads you up onto a wooden platform. "Mystery Hill was built like a huge clock," he says. "This modern platform stands at the hub—and all around the rim are triangular standing stones. They mark the exact location of the sunrise on ancient festival days."

Turn to page 56.

Your horse gallops across the open country and through an opening in a bank of tall hills. Before you is a wide valley with a strange green hill at its center. A spiral path climbs the hill, winding round and round it like a giant grass staircase. Mystery takes you up.

The hilltop is grassy and open, except for one strange, bumplike building. It's round and made of stones, much like the structures at Mystery Hill. You dismount and walk all around the stone, but you don't see an opening. Yet when you get back to the front, a low doorway is there.

Out steps a woman with cascading dark hair. She looks neither old nor young.

"Hello," you say. The woman nods. "I'm looking for a place called the Island of the Heroes," you continue. "A man called Merrill told me to find him there."

"You must take the ferry across the bay," says the woman, sweeping her hand out toward a body of water in the distance. "Then you must choose: Either climb the mountains or go around them by boat. Either way, you are sure to be tested."

Turn to page 62.

Turn to page 7

You've got to try to get home, and the crystal is your best chance.

"I'm going up there," you tell Merrill.

The old man nods. "You have earned the chance," he says. "Now you must earn the morning."

The climb is hard—very hard. Hauling yourself up, rock after rock, you scrape a knee and exhaust your limbs. You're afraid to look down the steep cliff. The gray sea churns and pounds below.

But you make it. Up here is the tiniest shelter, just a crevice of rock. You wedge yourself in and lie there, listening to the growling in your empty stomach.

So begins the longest, coldest, hungriest night of your life. All you can do is huddle against the cold rock. The frigid wind howls and moans all around. You lie there remembering everything that's happened on this incredible journey. Just when you think the night will never end, you glimpse the first glow of dawn.

Turn to page 119.

52

You and Tomah sit in blackness for hours. It's hard to tell how long. After a long while, you hear people moving about outside. Now you hear chanting—the same chanting that, at dawn yesterday, began the ceremony of sacrifice.

Then, like a flash of light in the darkness, it hits you. The white-robed men have convinced the Abenaki that only new sacrifice, new blood —controlled by the robed men—can bring on the sunrise! That's the secret of their tyranny: They and their "voice" pretend to have magic power over the dawn.

If only you can get that axe—you can prove it isn't so.

Suddenly the rock blocking the entryway is shoved aside. You crawl for it, hoping to bolt free—but as you emerge, several hands grab you and shove you to the ground. Quickly your hands and feet are bound with thick, ropelike strands. You're dragged across the ground. Behind you the same thing is happening to Tomah.

Turn to page 99.

You stoop to help Nyall. You tug hard at his struggling form. But the chieftain tenses in agony, and you realize it's no use. You can't get him out. You've got to think of something else.

You look up to see a man in rough clothes gripping a round wooden shield. His huge body blocks the sun, and you know he's a Saxon even as he lifts his battle-axe and brings the heel of it down at your head.

Turn to page 10.

54

"Who *are* you?" you ask Merrill. "And what am I doing here? I mean, why me?"

Merrill's blue eyes sparkle. "To find out, you must choose. As for me, I am a guide, just as I told you before."

You frown. That wasn't much help.

"The battle begins with the sunrise," the old man says. "You must decide quickly."

If you carry the standard into battle, you may be able to help the brave Britons conquer their invaders this last, most important time. Or you could go serve the legendary Arthur himself.

*If you choose to bear the standard,
turn to page 6.*

*If you go to Arthur,
turn to page 16.*

You and the Green Man cross a range of wind-chafed peaks. The side you've come up is green meadow and fir forest—yet the far side is brown and barren. Rocky slopes descend to parched valleys. Nothing seems to grow—nothing.

You stand on the ridge with the Green Man.

"My realm ends here," he says.

"Why is everything down there so dry and brown?" you ask.

"Because spring hasn't come," the Green Man answers.

"For how long?"

"For a long time."

"Then how do the people eat?"

"Mostly they fish. But now the fish are nearly gone."

The Green Man shakes your hand. "Remember what I said," he tells you. You promise to try. He turns and descends back to the green country of spring. You start down the other side.

Turn to page 63.

You peer out from the platform. About forty yards away in each direction stands a granite pillar. Each tip seems to puncture a spot on the hilly horizon.

"What were those festival days?"

Merrill recites them as his arm moves like a hand around the ancient clock. "There was the winter solstice, or shortest day of the year. Then the time when the year enters its dark half—when we celebrate Halloween. The summer solstice is the longest, brightest day. And in between is the most important time of all—the dawn of May Day, when the sun and its warmth return after the long, dark winter." He pauses. "May Day is tomorrow."

As he finishes, Merrill turns toward you. Again his blue eyes fasten onto yours.

Somehow you know that tonight you must come back to Mystery Hill.

Turn to page 8.

58

"I'll go to the time of the Great Heroes—whatever that is," you tell Merrill. You're wondering if this is just a dream.

But when the old man hands you the crystal, its cool, smooth sides and broken edges are solid in your fingers. Would it feel so real in a dream?

"Now comes the moment," Merrill says. "I must guide your hands."

His old fingers are strong as they grasp the backs of your hands. Merrill lifts your hands and the crystal, sighting down your arm until the crystal is lined up with the tip of a standing stone. You're pointing straight at the glow that is now spreading up the sky.

Dawn is breaking. The skyline is a combusting orange-red. As you hold the crystal straight out ahead of you, you see it start to take on the same colors. The clear rock turns rosy-orange, as if a fire is lighting inside; and now it's warm—really warm—it's almost too hot to—

"Now!" Merrill's voice commands.

The brilliant rim of the May Day sun pierces the sky above the distant hills. An incredible energy flashes from the sun through the crystal down your arm, and surges inside you.

"Hold on!" Merrill commands, as the hills and trees around you fade. Then there's only the brilliant light of dawn.

When you begin to see landscape around you again, everything looks different.

Turn to page 33.

This isn't a place of mystery. It's a place of terror—of strange men who pretend to speak from stones, frightening the people, demanding human blood at dawn.

The man's hands push you down.

You've got to escape! If you act fast, you may be able to break loose and scramble into that stone chamber. Maybe you can expose the person behind the voice. Break the bloody spell of these cruel rituals.

Or you can bolt for the woods. Will the native people help you? They might—or they might not.

If you try to enter the secret chamber,
turn to page 98.

If you bolt for the woods,
turn to page 37.

Unsure, you pick up the horn. Merrill smiles, but sadly. Putting the horn to your lips, you start to blow.

A long, deep, rich sound emerges. It fills the great stone room. You blow and blow until the air in your lungs is exhausted—and still you try to keep blowing, afraid to stop. When finally you must stop, when the sound is dying, you fall slowly to the floor. You're falling asleep, but not the strange sleep of Arthur and the other heroes. You must wake up, you tell yourself . . . Wake up.

You're awake. The wooden floor is hard but warm from the sun.

Wood? Sun?

You sit up straight. You're on the platform at Mystery Hill. Did you dream the whole thing?

You feel something hard in your pocket. You reach in and pull out the crystal. So it *did* happen!

As you start to reconstruct your strange journey, you feel a familiar grumble in your stomach. You decide to go try that snack bar.

The End

62

You're not sure what she means, but you thank her anyway. As you turn Mystery toward the bay, the woman speaks once more. "Make your choice before you reach the bay. The ferryman is kind, but he is a busy man. He won't stand around and wait for you to decide." Then she turns back toward the strange stone shape on the hilltop. The small doorway in it reappears —and from deep within you hear weird, surging sounds. Maybe it's the wind. Yet it seems to come from inside the hill itself.

The woman enters the opening. It disappears. The groaning stops.

Eager to get off this bizarre hilltop, you climb back on Mystery. But you'll heed the strange woman's advice. You could get some much-needed rest if you go by ship, but the mountains aren't that high; you might make better time crossing on foot. What should you tell the ferryman?

If you plan to tell him to take you to the mountain path, turn to page 96.

If you want him to take you around the mountains by water, turn to page 18.

Soon you come to a river, whose water runs deep and brown. You see a tiny boat with two women in it, fishing.

You call to the women in the boat. "Hello! Can you bring us across?"

"Our boat is too small for you and the horse," one woman calls back. "Another boat may come tomorrow. Follow the pathway back up the hill and you will find a great hall where you can stay the night."

You just came *down* that hill, you think. And there wasn't any great hall. But you and Mystery climb back up the hill anyway.

When you reach the top, you are amazed at what you find.

Turn to page 84.

You wake up. You're staring at rocks.

Your whole body aches. You're wet and cold. The rocks come into focus: They're the stones of the riverbed.

Are you drowned?

No. The river rushes past a few feet away. You're on dry ground.

You raise yourself painfully. You must have been washed up by the river. But where's Mystery?

You stand up and look downstream. The river surges through a narrow valley between the mountains. The horse is gone. Drowned? You wonder if you'll ever know.

Then you panic—the crystal!

You had it gripped in your hand, you remember, when you hit the rocks and went under.

The river has it now. It's gone.

You sit down miserably on the rocks. You're lost in wild, barren mountain country. Even your sword and shield are gone.

But you can't give up. There must be some people—a village, perhaps—around here somewhere. Maybe you can work for food and shelter. Maybe you can fish.

Your wet sneakers squeak as you begin walking upstream to an uncertain future, 1,500 years in the past.

The End

66

Openmouthed, you turn to look at the body. But it is not lying on the grass. The booted feet are still standing. You gaze up the muscular green legs, past the dark green tunic, and there is the Green Man—head and all. His neck isn't even cut.

He grins. "It grows back," he says.

As you drop the sword in amazement, he roars with laughter.

Turn to page 105.

You realize that without a standard to follow, dozens of soldiers will not know what to do, so you stand nobly, proudly, holding the flag of the golden rooster—symbol of dawn, of a new day —high and straight. You try not to look at the man pinned beneath you, nor at the crazy pounding and slashing that is pressing incredibly close all around.

You don't see the sword that fells you. It happens so fast you don't even know if it was a Saxon's or a Briton's. You just feel warm suddenly, and then everything is quiet.

The End

"Tell Mordred," Arthur instructs you, "that we will not meet on the sacred ground of Cammlatt. Tell him our forces will gather on the Strand of the Lion, in Cornwall. We shall meet there and we shall"—he spits out the word—"talk. And God help us if we do more."

Merrill bows to Arthur. You do the same. Lost in dark thought, the great leader nods.

Merrill leads you out of the tent.

"Who is Mordred?" you ask. "What's going on?"

"While we journey, I will explain," he says.

You both climb on the horse. Merrill spurs it hard, and suddenly the woods are rushing past.

Turn to page 30.

The battle's screams and shrieks echo wildly around you. You must help the fallen chieftain, and you must act fast—before any Saxons notice he's down and helpless.

Your orders were to keep the flag high and close to Nyall. You could rush toward him now, and maybe you should. But you have no weapons. If you go to Nyall, will his fighters see the gold rooster and come to his aid? Or will you and he both just be killed?

Perhaps instead you should try to rally Nyall's fighters yourself. You heard his battle cry: "Warriors of Avalon!" You could shout it yourself and wave the flag. His fighters are somewhere within the crush of flailing and smashing men just a few yards from you. Maybe they can save Nyall if you can get their attention.

Both choices seem almost hopeless—but either way, you must act now.

*If you rush to Nyall,
turn to page 13.*

*If you try to rally his warriors,
turn to page 39.*

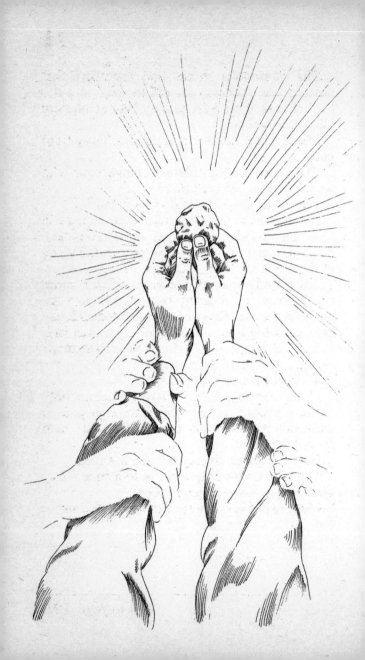

The mysterious stones and chambers that amazed you yesterday still call to you.

"I choose the Dawn of May Day at Mystery Hill," you say.

Merrill's face pales. He steps back, away from you.

"Then you'll have different companions," he says. "That is not my time."

"Not your time? What do you mean?"

But Merrill is fading. Now vague figures in long, pale robes take shape around you. Suddenly you experience a feeling of dread. You try to break away, to run, but you can't.

The ghostly figures encircle you. Their hands clutch yours, imprisoning the crystal in your fingers. As the sun slips above the distant hill, the pale, gripping hands point your crystal upward, straight at the sunlight. The clear stone glows orange, then red—deep red.

It's burning hot in your hands.

"No," you say. "I don't want to. Let me go!"

But a strange power surges through you. A wave of light and heat overwhelms you—then everything fades.

Now the hands that grip yours are real.

You look up into the faces of four men. They wear rough, ivory-colored robes.

Mystery Hill is still here. But it's not the same.

Turn to page 107.

"I need to cross these mountains," you tell the Green Man. "I need to reach the Island of the Heroes. Can you take me there?"

"No," the Green Man says. His voice is full and soft. "In this half of the mountains, I hold the power. I can bring you safely through my domain. But reaching that island is another matter."

"So you know about it!"

"I do." He nods. "Now, answer me. Have you ever seen a man such as me?"

Swallowing, you shake your head.

He smiles. "Then cut off my head."

You stare. "What?"

The Green Man speaks calmly. "Lift that sword you are gripping and swing it with all your strength at my neck. Cut off my head—if you can."

Your mind is racing. Cut off his head? If you kill the Green Man you might never get through the mountains.

But he has told you to do it. If you need his guidance, how can you start by disobeying him? You're sure this is a test—but what's the answer?

If you decide not to cut off the Green Man's head, turn to page 117.

If you swing your sword, turn to page 114.

In the morning, after a breakfast of oatmeal porridge, you lead Mystery to the water's edge. The ferryman is waiting for you, by a broad sort of rowboat. He laughs when you ask him if the boat can take the horse. "Well, I suppose we'll find out!" The boat tips and almost capsizes as Mystery steps in, but finally it grows steady. You climb in, and the ferryman rows you across the gray, lapping waters of the bay. On the other side you see green meadows rising to tall, craggy peaks. The mountains loom larger and taller as you come near shore.

You wonder how you'll ever reach the island beyond.

The ferryman directs you. "Follow the path from the ferry landing up over the first mountain pass. Beyond it continue down, down, and down until you find the Grove of the Green Man."

"The . . . Green Man?"

"You'll know him," says the ferryman, grinning, "when you see him."

Turn to page 88.

74

You urge Mystery into the fast-moving brown water. The horse enters, and soon the water is up to its flanks. Your legs are wet. Now Mystery is swimming. The horse's legs work against the steady current.

But the river is too powerful. You're beginning to move downstream. Mystery's head jerks, struggling to stay upright. Now you're sweeping along fast. Looking ahead, you see water bubbling around what must be submerged rocks.

Suddenly panicked, you think of the crystal. No matter what, you've got to hold on to it! You reach into your pocket. Suddenly you're cascading into a rapids of surging water.

When you hit it you're tumbling, head in the water, light and darkness rolling end over end. You reach out to protect yourself, to grab something, to find Mystery, and your body hits something hard.

You're badly hurt. You're going under.

Turn to page 65.

The soldiers carry Arthur along the shore of the tiny island.

"Let the procession go first," Merrill tells you.

You two wait while the sorrowing warriors bear their dying chieftain around the edge of the tall, rocky knob that occupies nearly all of this tiny island.

Merrill studies you with deep blue eyes. "This is the Island of the Heroes, the place beyond death," he says. "It is a place of legend—almost no one living ever reaches it. Do you think all these things would have happened to you if you did not have a destiny here?"

"But . . . I didn't ask to come. I didn't ask for any destiny. If I follow," you ask, "will I ever get home?"

"It depends."

"On what?"

"Very soon, you will see. But first you have another choice to make. This is a magical place, and you have shown much courage to get here. If you climb to the top of this peak, and if you can last a night there, at dawn you may use your crystal."

"To get home?"

Go on to the next page.

"That is all I can tell you. If, instead, you choose to come with me, a greater destiny may await."

You might be able to get home if you use your crystal. But what if it takes you somewhere else? And what does Merrill mean by "a greater destiny"? Is it worth the risk?

If you climb the mountain, turn to page 51.

If you follow Merrill, turn to page 92.

You decide to fight now, while you're still close to shore.

"No thief will reach that island," you declare as you draw your Saxon sword.

The man looks surprised and gazes sadly at your sword. You step forward—but you're not used to the boat's motion, and you stumble. Nimbly the man of the water steps aside. As you fall, he grabs your sword and uses it.

It happens so fast. He steps toward you, sure-footed in the swaying boat, and now the sword's handle is in your belly and you're staring at the blood that's covering his hand. Amazed, you look up.

The sailor looks sadly at you. "You ought to have trusted me," he says. "I wasn't what you thought."

But it's too late. You stagger backward and fall overboard.

The water is cold. It's dark. You're sleepy.

The End

The men wear belted tunics like yours, of every color in the rainbow. Over them many have strapped on gleaming breastplates of silver and bronze, some simple and some in elaborate designs. They carry long, polished swords and heavy battle-axes. Many sit on horses, whose coats are softly brushed. Others stand and lean against their weapons and their long, narrow metal shields.

Among the men are pennants of all colors on long poles, some bearing the figures of eagles, swords, or lions.

"These are the warriors of ancient Britain," Merrill says. "Long ago they were powerful— then for four hundred years their nation was ruled by the Roman Empire. Now Rome has crumbled, and its legions are gone from this island. So Britain has been invaded by Saxons, strong and ruthless fighters from eastward across the northern sea. All these brave warriors have gathered to battle the invaders under one great chieftain."

"Who's that?"

"His name is Arthur," Merrill says. "Now look."

Go on to the next page.

The old man leads you to the edge of the forest. At your feet a wide slope leads steeply downward to a cleft marked by a rough road. Beyond it open land rises to a range of bald, snowy mountains.

You hear a strange sound—a slow, rough pounding. It's coming from somewhere up the road that runs beneath you.

"Those are the Saxons," Merrill says. "They pound on their shields."

Turn to page 12.

You're not sure this is a good idea, but you're going to offer this red-haired woman the crystal.

You reach into your pocket and pull it out.

The hush seems even deeper now. Everyone watches you. Approaching the woman's bed, you say unsurely, "Is it possible you've been missing this?"

You hold out your hand and slowly open it. The woman's eyes widen.

"The fire stone," she whispers. "You have returned it to us!"

She holds out her hand. You place the crystal on her slim palm. She fits it into the gold-fingered setting around her neck.

Is it possible her hair begins to glow a deeper, fuller red? Surely the woman's face gains color —it seems to flush. Her voice grows full of life and joy as she sits up and announces to the company:

"The fire stone is in its place!"

Now everyone rises and crowds around, every single person craning to look, pointing and talking happily, all at once. You smile, though a little sadly. Have you given up your only way back?

As if from nowhere, a great feast appears: fat, golden-roasted birds and steaming stews with warm bread. Surrounded by laughter, singing, and merriment, you eat and drink till you're full and heavy as a stone. Sometime during the party, you fall asleep.

Turn to page 97.

A tall doorway stands before you. Surrounding the doorway is the front of a long, massive building made of huge timbers. Light flickers through the windows.

You tie Mystery to a post by the doorway and step in. Inside, torches blaze along the walls of a large room. Up high, dark, carved beams cross its length. Many people are sitting silently at long tables. They all look at you expectantly.

Your sneakers make the only sound as you walk down the center aisle between the tables. At the end, lit by torches, is a bed. On it lies a young woman with pale red hair, propped up against pillows. She is beautiful—or she was. Now her face is drawn and colorless. She looks weak and sick.

"We welcome you here," the woman says in a thin voice. From her heavy necklace hangs a large setting of gold shaped like tiny fingers, as if to hold a particular stone. But the gold fingers are empty.

Right away you know that the shape they form exactly matches the crystal in your pocket.

Turn to page 43.

"Mordred," says Merrill, "Arthur is deeply angry that you have occupied this fortress, which is his own."

"It is my own now," Mordred answers defiantly, crossing his arms.

Merrill looks at you expectantly. Suddenly you remember your purpose. "Arthur has charged me to deliver this message," you say. "Briton must not quarrel with Briton at this perilous time. He asks that you and your warriors meet him and his forces on the Strand of the Lion, in Cornwall, in eight days' time."

Mordred looks at you with contempt. But he nods. "We will meet Arthur."

As you and Merrill stride from the hall, you ask: "What's a strand, anyway?"

"It is what you call a beach," says Merrill. "You have served Arthur well—so far. But now comes the most dangerous day of all."

Turn to page 27.

You step up to the sword and pull it from its scabbard. Instantly you feel a surge of power. It's as if you and the sword are one.

Merrill smiles and spreads his arms.

"You have made the warrior's choice," he says. "You are worthy to join our heroes. I, Merlin the Wizard, commend you to the sleep of the ages."

Merlin! So *that's* who he really is.

You have so many questions. But you're already sleepy. Hazily you step to the stone bed and climb upon it. Laying your sword at your side, you cross your arms.

The last thing you notice is lamplight, flickering up the sides of the gray stone walls in this strange, magical chamber.

There will be no questions or answers—not just now. There is only sleep—sleep that will last until the time when the old heroes, including you, are needed again.

The End

A well-worn path crosses the meadows at the foot of the peaks. Then it climbs steeply, switching back and forth until you and Mystery finally reach the pass.

Ahead you see ridge after ridge of rough mountains. Some are bare and round as a bald man's head; others have dense forests that give way to jagged peaks. You can't see the end of the mountains.

Following the ferryman's directions, you and Mystery climb down, down, down. You go from open, windswept high country through tall, shadowing pines. When you finally reach the bottom, you are standing in a grove of apple trees.

The grove is a peaceful, quiet place, and the trees are alive with white spring blossoms. You wonder if this is the right place, when someone —or something—steps from the trees.

You shudder and grip your Saxon's sword. Before you stands a tall, strong-looking man wearing soft boots and a leather tunic. He is completely green. His tunic and boots are green, his belt is green, the sword stuck in his belt is green—and he himself is the color of a leaf when you see the sun through it: bright, living green. So is his hair. Even his eyes are deep green.

The man smiles at you. His teeth are green.

"Set your feet on the grass," he says.

You do so, still gripping your sword.

Turn to page 72.

Seeing a movement, you lift your head. Standing right in front of you is a boy, deerskin clad, about your age.

The boy gazes seriously at you. His loose, pale yellow shirt is decorated with small shells sewn in a curling pattern. He wears moccasins. The boy points to himself.

"Tomah," he says.

His name!

You tell him yours.

He says no more, but motions for you to follow.

Turn to page 42.

Watching with Tomah, you point to the sacrifice table. You motion to the Abenaki men, then make a chop, as if with an axe. You shrug, to ask Tomah: "Do they kill your people?"

Tomah nods. Then he makes a series of motions that you struggle to understand. He points to himself, then holds up two fingers. Now he points to the sacrifice table and makes the chop. Again he holds up two fingers—but this time, very sadly, he folds one down.

Your heart fills with sadness and rage. Tomah had a brother—maybe a twin. The robed men killed him.

Tomah points to himself and chops again.

Motioning quickly, you say: "They want to kill you, too, don't they? That's why you were in the woods. You escaped, just like me."

Tomah nods.

But you still don't get it. *Why?* Why do they do this? And how can you stop them?

Suddenly you get an idea.

You point to the robed men, then make the motion of sleeping. Tomah nods.

You pretend to sneak along, very quietly— then point to the complex. *Tonight,* you are saying, *when everyone sleeps, we go there.* You make the chopping motion—then you pretend to grab something.

The axe, you're saying. *We get the axe.*

Light dawns on Tomah's face. He nods. *Yes!*

Turn to page 44.

You realize you may never get home; yet this greater destiny is calling you. "I'll go with you," you tell Merrill.

Merrill leads you around the mountain's edge. On the other side, the mountain drops off to a steep cliff. This back half of the island is flat and open to the sea. It's barren. There's nothing here.

"Where are the men? Where's Arthur?"

Merrill doesn't answer. He walks to the base of the cliff. You follow.

A doorway in the cliff is open. You're sure it wasn't there a moment ago. Merrill stoops and enters, motioning for you to follow.

Inside is an enormous, high room, lit by flickering lamps. The walls are gray rock, and you realize the whole inside of the mountain is hollow.

Blinking, you look around.

On a bed of stone before you lies Arthur, his arms folded. But his wound is gone. The blood has disappeared. His tunic is clean and whole.

Behind him are many more stone beds. Each one holds a British warrior, each dressed in battle garb. They don't look dead. They look asleep.

"Yes," says Merrill, as if reading your thoughts. "They are asleep."

Go on to the next page.

He leads you to a table. On it are a sword of silver and a horn of brass. Beside it is an empty stone bed.

"These are the heroes of Arthur's day," Merrill says. "They lie here asleep until some future time when their bravery is needed most. You have a chance to join them, but you must choose correctly. You must either blow the horn or draw the sword."

You know he isn't going to tell you anything more, so you don't ask. But you wonder what the horn and sword mean. Is one the way to get home? Is the other the key to a greater destiny? You'll never know until you make your choice.

If you blow the horn, turn to page 60.

If you draw the sword, turn to page 87.

Your journey is easy and pleasant, for once. Traveling west toward the sunset, you spend one night in a friendly farm village. The next day, smelling salt air, you round a bend and behold the great, gray-watered ocean.

Sticking up straight across the water, perhaps half a mile away, is a small hump of an island. A little mountain seems to cover just the back half, hiding the far side of the island.

A sailboat approaches from the distance. It's steering right for you. It's shaped almost like a big canoe, with a square sail and both ends upraised. It slides to a stop before you.

Merrill leans out from the boat's wooden rail.

"Climb on," he says.

On the rough deck of the ship, two warriors weep as they tend to a bleeding man. He wears a green tunic, threaded with gold and soaked with blood. Somehow you know he is the great King Arthur.

"How was he wounded?" you ask.

"In a battle of Briton against Briton," says Merrill. "A terrible, terrible waste of a fight."

The sail fills. The boat surges out to the open water.

"Are we sailing to the island?"

"Yes," says Merrill. "We bring Arthur to his rest."

"What about me?" you ask hesitantly.

"You have one final choice to make," says the old guide as the boat pulls up to land.

Turn to page 76.

You've decided you'll climb over the mountains. You set off in search of the ferryman.

At the edge of the bay is a building made of timbers, with a shed beside it. You see light flickering in the building, so you dismount and enter.

Inside, a stout, friendly man with a sandy beard is drawing dark cider from a wood barrel.

"I'm looking for the ferryman," you say.

"I'm he," says the man. "And I'm the innkeeper in the evening. You'll stay here tonight, and I'll bring you across in the morning."

So you stay. You're grateful for the warm meal and hot cider you're given. Mystery is fed and watered in the shed, and you sleep soundly on a bed of packed straw.

Turn to page 73.

Sometime later you awake with a start. It's dawn. The people are gone.

Behind the woman's bed is a round, open window. Through it you see the glow of sunrise.

The red-haired woman sits facing the window and the rising sun. She holds up the crystal, its necklace hanging from her hand.

There's a humming like bees in the room. Where is it coming from? Maybe from the crystal. You're not sure.

The woman—her hair is flaming red now—holds the clear stone high as the sun's crimson edge emerges outside. You remember the dawn at Mystery Hill. Now, as the light catches the crystal and kindles inside it, you wonder what will happen this time.

But you're not prepared for what does happen.

Turn to page 111.

You've got to prove it's a trick.

The robed men don't expect you to resist, so you break free easily. You dash through the low entrance and into the darkness of the stone chamber.

You feel along the wall: all smooth stones. But now there's a space. You reach inside and grab a foot. Two feet!

There's a struggle—but you're bigger and stronger than these men of ancient times. You haul the man out by his robe. He tries to escape, elbowing you hard and scrambling away in the dirt. But you grab an arm and hold on. Bracing your legs on the stone wall, you slide outside.

You stand up in the dawn light and pull the man out behind you.

The crowd in deerskin gasps, murmurs angrily, then turns and bolts into the woods. It worked! You've exposed the secret voice—and broken the spell of terror.

Some of the robed men chase the people. But now the man with the bronze axe rushes toward you. There's murderous fury in his eyes as he raises the axe to swing it at you.

Turn to page 15.

You glimpse a man slipping into the chamber. In a moment, the same voice comes from beneath the table again. The chanting grows louder and louder.

You are dragged to the table of sacrifice. Just as the light spreads above the hilltop to the east, the white-robed man raises the bronze axe. You see it flash with the first light of day, just before it drops.

Four thousand years from now, this place will have tour guides and a snack bar. But you've learned the secret—the cruel, bloody lie—behind the building of Mystery Hill. And the truth, you know in this last moment of your life, will die with you.

The End

The Saxons must be drunk. Two of them tangle up in the weeds and fall, cursing and laughing in a strange language. The third stumbles onto the Roman road ahead of you. He crouches, raising his sword to block your way.

But he's not ready for Mystery. The Saxon's eyes widen as the horse sails into him, knocking him into some tangled brambles. His sword and shield go clattering up the road.

The horse stops. You don't know why, but then you see that you've paused by the Saxon's weapons. Should you pick them up? You might need them.

You dismount and retrieve the weapons. Hearing shouts, you look back. The first two Saxons are stampeding toward you, waving their swords. But there's no point in fighting them. Surely you'd be killed. And somehow you know that your purpose here has nothing to do with the Saxon invaders anyway.

You hop back up on Mystery. You're about to kick the horse's flanks when you realize there's no need. You're already gliding forward.

You look back at the Saxons. They stand openmouthed, watching you, the burning village and smoking hill fort behind them. You hoist the stubby sword in mock salute to the new rulers of England.

Turn to page 49.

You've got to hold on to the crystal.

You don't ask about the necklace. You don't mention the crystal. After a short period of silence, everyone in the hall seems to sigh. Weakly the woman says, "We have precious little food to offer. But you must share what we have."

The whole evening in the hall is sad and subdued. Some bowls of fish soup are brought out, and everyone is given a little in a wooden cup. The soup is thin and meager. After eating you curl up in a corner of the hall and go to sleep.

You wake up early and slip out the door. Mystery is there. You climb on and quietly ride away, back down to the river.

There is no boat this morning. The path ends at the water. You hope that Mystery can swim you across.

Turn to page 74.

You must obey Arthur's order. You close your eyes and hope the snake passes on.

But you feel a sharp sting in your ankle. The adder's poison works almost instantly, and you fall to the ground, your body clenching in violent convulsions.

Blinded by the poison, you'll never know that your movements startle Mordred's forces, and they charge. The battle that takes Arthur's life begins with your own death.

The End

But the deerskin people don't move—amazed, they just watch you run past. As you sprint among the birch and maple trees, you hear men yelling behind you. But the shouts fade. Is anyone following?

You stop and listen. No footsteps.

Breathless, you lean back against a tree. You got away!

But now what?

These woods look pretty much the same as they do in present-day New Hampshire. The early-spring ground is spongy with last summer's fallen brown leaves. You wonder how far in the past you've come. If this is really the Dawn of Mystery Hill, that would be some four thousand years ago—the Bronze Age.

Now you remember something. The executioner's axe was bronze.

So somehow, white-skinned men *did* come here long before Columbus—even before the Vikings. Somehow they have power over the deerskin people, who watch their sacrifices and do nothing. Are they, too, victims of these ritual killings?

More important: What will you do now?

Turn to page 89.

"Why can you—I mean, how can you do that?" you ask.

The Green Man roars again, his deep laughter echoing against the rising cliffs all around. "I am of the earth—I regrow myself," he says. "Are you surprised when the leaves and the grass regrow themselves in the spring?"

"No."

"Then why be shocked that I can?"

"But you're a person," you say. "Aren't you?"

The Green Man guffaws. "*Am* I?"

Now he grows serious. "You met my challenge," he says. "I will bring you through my realm." He summons a stallion from somewhere in the apple grove. The tall horse's glossy coat is dark brown as new-turned earth. The Green Man mounts the stallion and urges it forward. He motions for you to follow.

You ride side by side. "I've got to reach the Island of the Heroes," you say to him. "It's the only way I can get home."

The Green Man looks at you. "Only one living person has ever gone to that island," he says.

"Who's that?"

The Green Man does not answer your question. "Remember this," he says. "Trust the mystery."

As you ride upward, deep into the mountain country, you wonder what he meant.

Turn to page 55.

106

You step up from the heap of dead warriors. It is amazing how nothing moves here—even the clouds in the sky are still. Did Arthur's men defeat the Saxons? Did they keep the invaders out of Scotland? Maybe you'll never know.

You must find this island. But how will you get there? You've got nothing.

You climb the hill. Your legs feel weary already.

At the top, you look back. The legendary last stand of Arthur's Britons against the Saxons is now nothing more than a silent tangle of dead men. You'll never forget the sight.

You turn and peer into the old woods. Merrill is gone. But there among the massive trees stands his horse.

Turn to page 26.

Instead of a modern wood platform, you're standing on a slab of stone. There's no fence around the complex. Instead of age-old and tumbled down, Mystery Hill looks unfinished and new, as if it's still being built.

The four men are shorter than you. They have long brown hair, close-cropped beards, and a haughty, commanding manner. One of them grips your arm and leads you from the stone slab to the center of the Mystery Hill complex. All around you can see people—a different sort of people. Instead of ivory robes, they wear long, simple shirts and narrow leggings made of soft, pale yellow deerskin. Many wear colorful decorations. They are smaller and darker skinned than the robed men. They must be the natives of these woods.

The people watch silently as you are led to a stone table. It's the one with the strange gutters cut around its rim. Those gutters—in fact, the whole table—are stained a dark brownish red.

The people are waiting expectantly for something. Is this part of the ancient festival?

It's still not quite dawn. The first glow of day is just spreading above the distant hill.

Everyone is watching you. Why?

Turn to page 34.

108

There is no dance or sweep to this battle. The men just crash into each other, cramming chest-to-chest, everyone hacking and stabbing in a wild and brutal mayhem. The narrow mountain cleft explodes with shouts and screams. All around you sunlight catches the clash of slashing swords and axes.

You stand on the slope, gripping your standard pole and staring at this terrible madness. You just want to run, and when a man falls in front of you, horribly wounded, you almost do turn and dash back up for the woods.

But you remember your task and the dancing eyes of the leader Nyall. You must prove yourself now by doing your job amid the battle's wild nightmare.

Looking around frantically, you spot the gold rooster on the flank of Nyall's rearing horse. You start to go to him just as his horse falls sideways and lands on its side with a sickening thud.

Nyall is pinned beneath the fallen horse. Blood pours from an awful gash in the horse's side. The young chief is trapped—and his face twists in agony. The horse's fall has crushed Nyall's leg.

As Nyall shoves at his dying horse, you gape at the enraged Saxons fighting just a few feet away. Nyall's men have been swallowed up in the battle. No one has come to the chieftain's side.

You've got to do something. But what?

Turn to page 69.

You and Merrill cross into Avalon, a broad, low valley surrounded on three sides by high hills and a wide bay to the west. In the valley's center is a grassy hill with a strange, wide pathway spiraling up it. And at one side of the valley rises another hill with a fortress on top.

Climbing that hill, you expect a grand storybook castle—but those, you guess, were built in later times. Arthur's Cammlatt is a large but simple hall built of wood. It is protected within tall banks of earth and rough timbers that ring the hilltop's edge.

Merrill strides boldly into the wood hall, with you beside him. Within waits a young chieftain in black robes with a close-cropped black beard. He, too, seems to know the old guide.

Turn to page 85.

The crystal glows as if on fire inside. Now the red glow is all around it—and all around the flaming-haired woman.

The place grows very warm. The humming is louder and louder. Now the place is on fire.

It's on fire—all around you! The wood timbers catch, smolder, and burst into flames. You leap up and shout at the woman—but the humming, very loud now, drowns your voice out completely.

The woman, her hair the color of fire, sits absolutely still and unafraid—yet her bed is roaring with fire, and the flames are spreading up the hall.

You stare at her, knowing you must run—but not understanding what's happening.

She smiles—and her voice comes to you.

I am of the fire, the voice says. *Sometimes there must be fire, to bring a new beginning.*

Her voice fades, and the flames engulf her. It may be too late for you to escape.

Turn to page 40.

112

The beach is filled with dying men. There are no enemies anymore. There is only disaster.

Two survivors lift a figure from the tangled mess. They carry the body toward the water— and you realize whose it is.

"Arthur!" you shout, and run toward the men.

The great leader lies by the shore, bleeding from a stab wound to his midsection. You know he's dying.

Merrill stands beside you. You look up to see a boat—some kind of sailboat, with both ends pointed and upraised. You didn't notice it before. It must have come in the fog.

Lovingly, silently, the men lift Arthur into the boat. They climb in after.

"Come," says Merrill. "This is the final chapter."

You climb into the boat, and it sails away from the awful scene.

"Where are we going?" you whisper to Merrill.

"To the Island of the Heroes," he says.

As the boat surges across the water, a great tiredness overwhelms you. You lie down on a wood bench and fall asleep.

When you wake up, the boat has landed.

Turn to page 76.

"A most important engagement is about to take place," the old man says. "You may play a role. But first, please—keep the crystal close to you, hidden in a safe place."

You look at the clear stone. It feels cool again. You put it in the pocket of your jeans.

"Do not lose that stone," Merrill says. "It got you here."

"Okay," you answer. "Can it get me home again?"

"Perhaps," Merrill answers—and he turns away.

You, Merrill, and the horse climb a long slope in the woods. You're wondering what he meant by an "engagement"—and what "role" you may play.

When you reach the crest, you stop short, astonished at what you see.

Among the old trees, the long ridge is crowded with men dressed for battle.

Turn to page 80.

114

"All right, I'll do it," you say. "But I'm not at all sure about this."

The Green Man says nothing. He spreads his strong legs a little, claps his hands on his green hips, and waits.

"Cut clean and hard," he says. "Strike with the sharp edge of the blade. Use all your strength."

"O . . . kay." You grip the Saxon's sword. You take a deep breath and look at the Green Man.

His neck is bare. He just stands there.

You rear back. This thick sword is heavy. You swing it from far back, blade turned so the weapon slices hard through the air and cuts right through the bright green neck of the Green Man.

His head tumbles clean off and thuds on the grass. You watch, hypnotized. The head rolls a little, then stops. In the sunlight, it quickly darkens and shrivels. Like an apple left on the ground, the Green Man's head turns brown. Now it's wrinkled, skinny, and finally dried up like a husk.

Turn to page 66.

116

The scrawny man shoves the boat away from the wood pier. His pursuer reaches the edge just as you're drifting away. He shakes his fist.

"Thief! Rodent! Pillager!" He lumbers back to shore and begins heaving stones at the boat.

Ping! Ponk! The stones thunk off the planks. You shield your head with your arms. But the skinny sailor only shrugs and goes to work hoisting his sail.

"A few hunks of bread and cooked meat—*pish*," he says. "Such a busy inn has plenty of those, but would that one give a crust to a poor man? We'd all starve first."

As he works, you look him over. He has a sharp face with a short, dark beard and hair. His little black eyes glint as he hoists the sail. He wears a shapeless cloak of rough wool. You wonder: *Is* he a thief, or what?

And where are you going?

Turn to page 35.

"I can't kill you—I need your help," you tell the Green Man.

He gazes calmly at you and shrugs.

"You have chosen not to trust the mystery," he says. "You must go now—on your own."

He turns from you and steps back into the grove. Among the white-blossoming trees, the Green Man vanishes.

"I wish people here wouldn't do that," you mutter as you turn to climb back on Mystery.

But the horse, too, is gone.

A cold shudder runs through you. You really *are* alone.

Lying on the ground is the Saxon's round shield. You pick it up. At least you have this, and the sword.

You begin picking your way up the path from the apple grove.

Turn to page 21.

Even if this man is a thief, you must trust him. After all, his was the boat that waited for you.

"I'll come along," you say.

The man nods. "My name is Sinnitt," he says. "I am of the water. I'll take you to your island."

Your island? What does he mean?

Sinnitt guides the little boat around a great thrust of mountainous land and over the gray water till you see a tiny island in the distance. As you approach the island, you spot a larger sailboat already moored near the shore. A small bare mountain on the rocky island hides the side that faces away from land.

Sinnitt draws the boat to shore. From the larger boat you see some men carefully unloading a limp figure in green and gold.

Sinnitt looks at you and nods.

"Go," he says.

You climb overboard and drop to the rocky shore. As you walk toward the group of men, you look back to wave. But Sinnitt and his boat are already sailing away. As the boat rounds the thrust again, it seems to disappear.

You trot ahead. Two men carry a brown-bearded man in a green and gold tunic that's badly stained with blood. At your side you hear a familiar voice.

"This is Arthur," says Merrill.

"He's dying," you say, "isn't he?"

"Yes. And now you must come and make your final choice."

Turn to page 76.

Standing atop the mountain, you fumble for the crystal in your pocket. You bring it out, but your numb fingers can't hold it. It rolls toward the edge of the cliff. You dive and save it just in time.

Now the dawn is coming. You stand, the wind whipping your hair, and hold up the crystal, gripping it firmly.

The sun catches the clear stone and turns it fiery orange and warm, then hot. The heat enters your fingers, surging down your arm. Then the world glows orange-red, and everything goes bright, like a silent explosion.

You shake your head. The wind is gone.

You look around at the wire fence and wooden platform of Mystery Hill. You take a deep breath and let it out slowly. Then you climb back over the fence, grab your bike, and head for home. That crystal's going to look pretty cool on your bookshelf.

The End

ABOUT THE AUTHOR

DOUG WILHELM is a free-lance writer and editor and the author of *The Forgotten Planet* and *Scene of the Crime* in Bantam's Choose Your Own Adventure series. He has traveled to many parts of the world, and his special interest in ancient mysteries led him to write *The Secret of Mystery Hill.* He currently lives in Montpelier, Vermont, and has a son, Bradley, who is almost seven years old.

ABOUT THE ILLUSTRATOR

TOM LA PADULA has illustrated *The Luckiest Day of Your Life, Secret of the Dolphins,* and *Scene of the Crime* in Bantam's Choose Your Own Adventure series. He earned his Bachelor of Fine Arts from the Parsons School of Design and his Master of Fine Arts from Syracuse University. For over a decade he has illustrated for national and international magazines, advertising agencies, and publishing houses. Tom is on the faculty of Pratt Institute, where he teaches a class in illustration. In 1992, his work appeared in the group show "The Art of the Baseball Card" at the Baseball Hall of Fame in Cooperstown, New York. Additionally, his pieces now grace several private collections, including that of the Johnson & Johnson corporation. Tom lives in New Rochelle, New York, with his wife, son, and daughter.